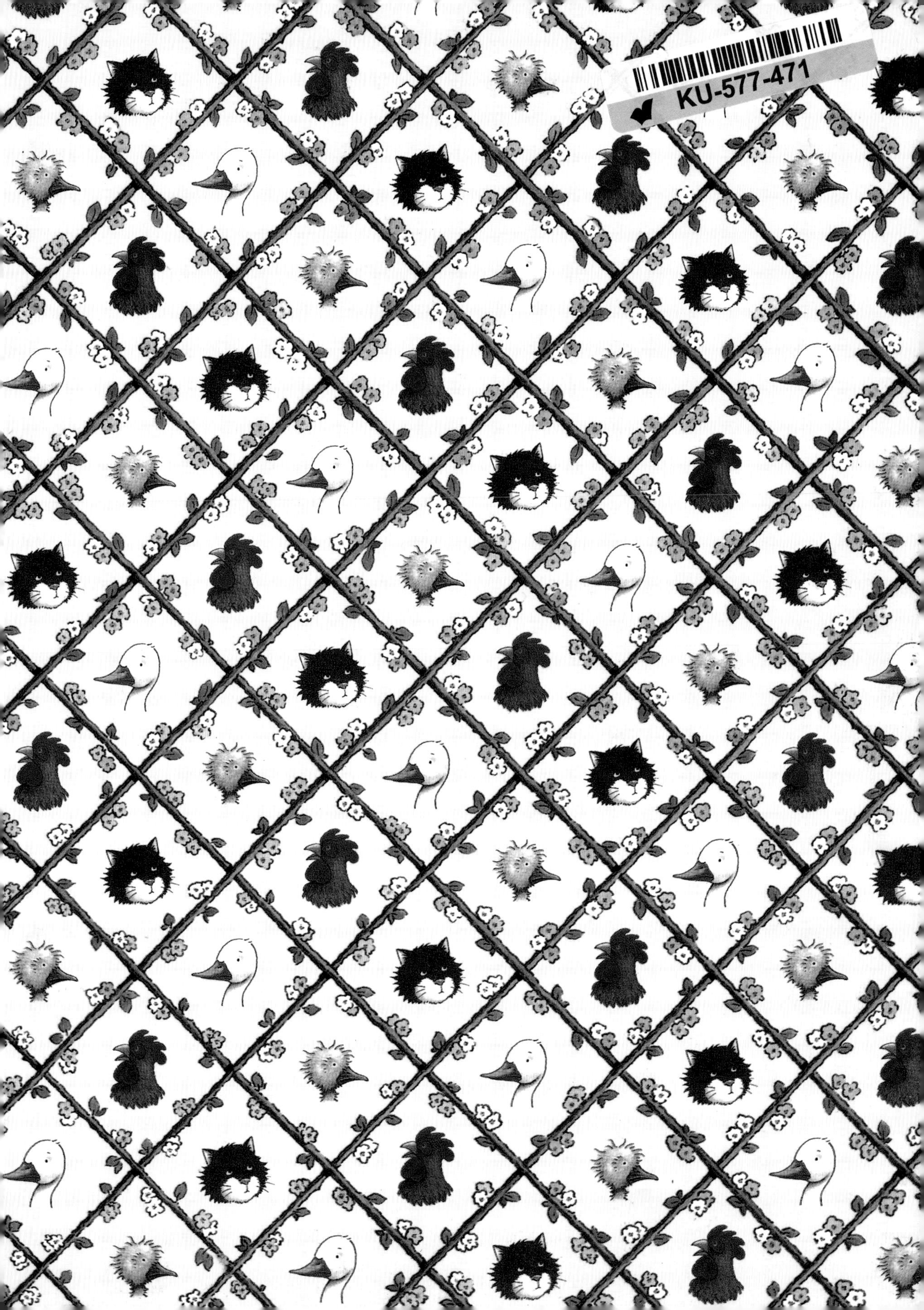

Jonathan Langley's version of
THE UGLY DUCKLING
is based on the original story
by Hans Christian Andersen.

First published in Great Britain by HarperCollins Publishers Ltd in 1991
First published in this edition in Picture Lions in 1996
7 9 10 8
Picture Lions is an imprint of the Children's Division, part of HarperCollins
Publishers Ltd, 77-85 Fulham Palace Road, Hammersmith, London W6 8JB.

ISBN: 0 00 664397 3

Printed in Hong Kong by Midas Printing Limited

The Ugly Duckling

Retold & Illustrated By
Jonathan Langley

PictureLions
An Imprint of HarperCollins*Publishers*

Once upon a time, on a dark and stormy night, a great wild wind blew down from the hills. It whistled through the woods and across the fields to the river where it blew a poor mother duck right out of her nest.

"Oh dear," she said, picking herself up, "I must get back to my eggs!"

She stumbled around in the dark until she found her nest then, exhausted, she settled down again on the eggs to keep them warm.

In the morning the storm had passed and the sun came up warm and bright. The mother duck awoke when she felt something move beneath her.

The eggs were rocking to and fro. She counted them, "One, two, three, four, five, six ... seven?" She had only laid six eggs but now there were seven, and one was much bigger than the rest.

"I don't remember that one," she said. "Seven eggs, I am a lucky duck!"

Soon, one by one, the smaller eggs broke open and out popped six pretty little yellow ducklings. But the biggest egg had not hatched.

The six ducklings gathered around the big egg and watched as the mother duck sat on top of it for a day and a night until the egg, at last, began to stir. Slowly it cracked open and out tumbled a big scruffy duckling with grey feathers and very big black feet.

"Oh my," said the mother duck, "you are a funny one!"

The other six ducklings were a little afraid of their new brother and scurried under the mother duck to hide. They peered out at the big grey duckling as he wobbled out of his shell, gazed around at the world and smiled.

"Oh well," said the mother duck, "he looks happy and healthy," and cuddled him to her with the other ducklings.

Next day the mother duck led her new family down to the river for a swimming lesson. The six little yellow ducklings scampered down the bank after their mother while the big grey duckling followed clumsily behind. One by one they jumped in the water. The yellow ducklings struggled and splashed but the grey duckling found his big feet very useful and he swam straight away. The other ducklings tried to keep up with him but the big duckling was much too fast.

"Oh well," said the mother duck, "he may not be a beauty but he can certainly swim."

One day the mother duck took her ducklings to visit some friends in the farmyard. The farm ducks were thrilled to see the new yellow ducklings.

"What little beauties!" they said, fussing around and patting them. Then they saw the big grey duckling.

"What is that?" said one old duck.

"What a strange awkward creature," said another.

The big grey duckling became shy and hid behind his mother but she was proud of all her offspring and urged him on saying, "And this is my big strong son."

The big duckling stuck out his chest and stepped forward but tripped over his feet and fell head first in a muddy puddle. The farm ducks all laughed, "Ha, ha, ha, what a mess!"

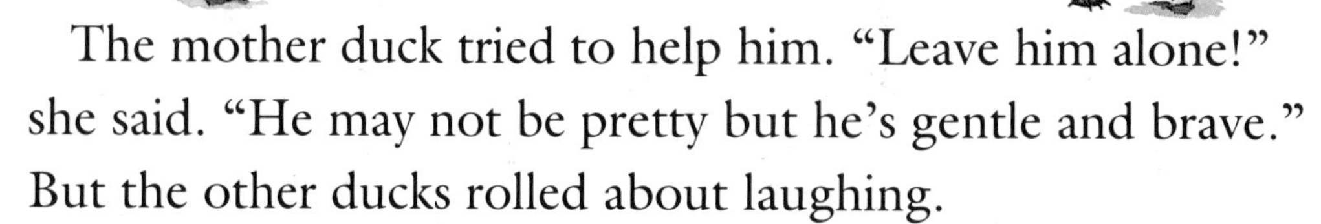

The mother duck tried to help him. “Leave him alone!” she said. “He may not be pretty but he’s gentle and brave.” But the other ducks rolled about laughing.

“Ha, ha, ha, what a clumsy cluck! What an ugly duckling!”

Other animals came over to see what the joke was. When the hens saw the big duckling they laughed too, and so did the pigs, and the sheep, and the cow, and the horse.

The duckling looked around at all the laughing animals and frowned.

"I don't belong here!" he said and ran out of the farmyard and away across the fields.

The duckling ran on and on until he came to the great marsh where the wild ducks live. He was tired and sat down to rest in a clump of reeds.

"I know I'm not little, yellow and fluffy like my brothers and sisters," he said to himself. "But I'm me! I may be scruffy and grey and I may have big black feet, but I'm as good as they are."

Three wild ducks were flying past and saw him sitting in the reeds.

"Look, there's a mumbling duckling with big feet!" said one and they all laughed.

The duckling looked up and stuck his tongue out at them, he didn't care. The wild ducks flew away laughing loudly. "See you again flipper feet," they called.

"I'll show them," said the duckling.

He fell asleep and dreamed he was with other ducklings just like himself, but suddenly – BANG! BANG! BANG! – the duckling awoke with a start. Men were shooting at ducks all around!

He put his wings over his head and tried to hide but then something came rushing towards him through the marsh – a huge dog with a big red tongue and sharp teeth!

The duckling jumped into a pool and hid under the water until the dog had gone.

"I don't belong here!" said the duckling. "This is a terrible place!" and he hurried away from the marsh.

As darkness fell he came to the big wood. Strange noises and shadows seemed to follow him as he waddled along the path through the tall trees.

"I don't belong here," he whispered.

Soon he came to a tumbledown cottage where a light shone from a window. The house belonged to an old woman who lived with her cat and a hen. The duckling was cold and tired and he could see it was warm inside, so he crept in through a crack in the door.

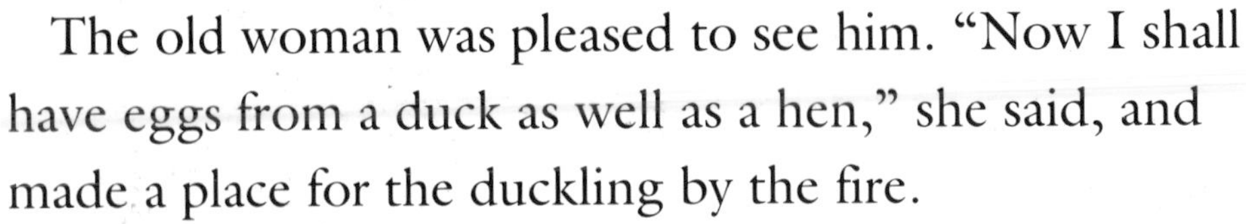

The old woman was pleased to see him. "Now I shall have eggs from a duck as well as a hen," she said, and made a place for the duckling by the fire.

When the old woman went to bed the cat and the hen cornered the duckling.

"Can you lay eggs?" said the hen.

"No," said the duckling, "but I can swim."

"Can you purr?" said the cat.

"No," replied the duckling, "but I can dive."

"Swim and dive indeed! You're no use to our mistress," they both said.

"I don't care!" said the duckling and waddled out of the door and into the night. "I don't belong here," he said.

The duckling journeyed on and on over hills and dales looking for a place to call home. Eventually he found a small lake where he lived on his own and no one bothered him.

Many weeks passed and the leaves on the trees turned from green to brown. The days were shorter and the duckling shivered through the long nights.

One evening, as the sun was setting, he heard a strange sound in the sky and looked up to see a flock of the most beautiful birds. They were magical white birds with great outstretched wings and long graceful necks.

One of them gave a strange cry that he seemed to understand and he wished he could go with them.

Soon the cold winds of winter blew and the lake, where the duckling lived, began to freeze. He swam round and round to keep warm but the water froze around his feet and he was stuck fast.

Next morning a kind farmer passed by and saw the duckling. He smashed the ice and carried the frozen bird home and put him by the fire to warm up. The duckling felt happy and safe but when the farmer's children came home they were noisy and frightened him.

He flapped his wings to try to get away from them and knocked over a bowl of milk. Their mother tried to catch him but he flew into the butter tub and then fell in the flour barrel. Milk, butter and flour were spilled all over the floor! The farmer shouted, the mother shouted, the children shouted too!

"I don't belong here!" said the duckling, and ran out of the door.

On and on he ran through the snow until he could run no more and there he curled up in a hollow and slept for the rest of the long cold winter.

He awoke beside a large lake with the sun on his back and the larks singing overhead. Spring had come at last. The grass was green, there was blossom on the trees, and he was feeling much stronger.

He wandered down to the water and swam away from the bank. He was enjoying himself when, from behind some tall rushes, sailed three of the beautiful white birds he had seen flying so high, and they were coming towards him. He thought they were going to call him names as most animals did so he puffed himself up ready for them, but instead they greeted him warmly.

"Hello brother, you are new to these parts."

The ugly duckling thought they were talking to someone else and bowed his head in confusion. Then he saw his reflection in the still water.

He was no longer scruffy, grey and clumsy. He was big and white and graceful and ... just like the beautiful birds who were talking to him!

"What am I?" he said to the three swans.

“Why you’re a swan, and a very handsome one too,” they replied.

“A swan, a swan! I’m not an ugly duckling, I’m a swan!” he cried.

The duckling swan lived happily ever after. The three older swans became his best friends and they swam and flew everywhere together.

One day he was flying over the riverbank when he saw his mother with a new family of ducklings (every one a duck this time). He flew down and told her his story. She was delighted with his good fortune and very proud of him. From then on, whenever she saw a swan flying high above her in the sky, she would say to her ducklings, or anyone else who would listen, "That's probably my son up there."

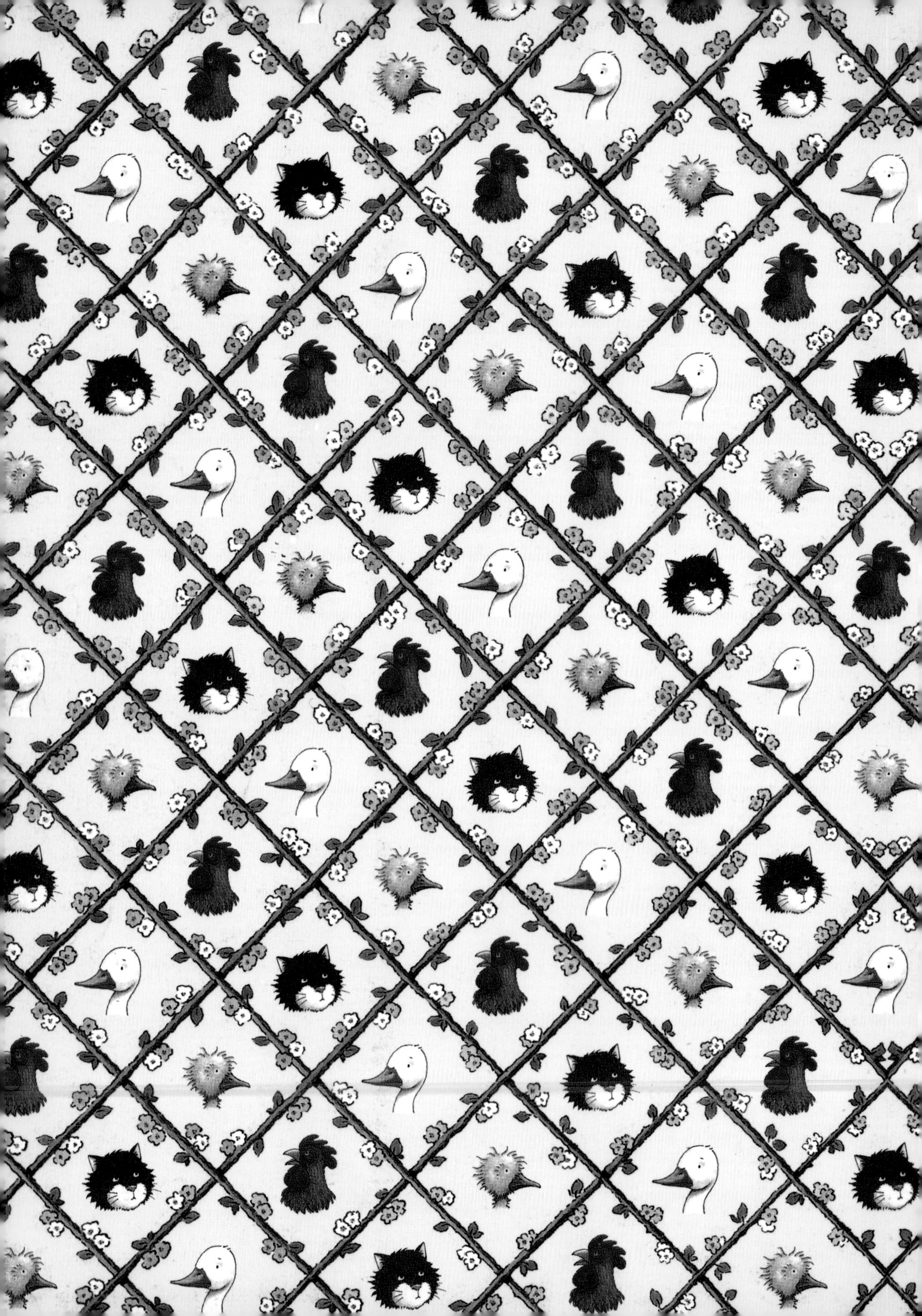